CW01081212

This book is dedicated to,
My sons for inspiring me,
My husband for supporting me,
My pets for unconditionally loving me.
Thank you for allowing me, to pursue me.

Always stay true to being you,

Shona

If I Could... Be a PET!

Written by Shona Darin   Illustrations by Anne Zimanski

If you brushed my
floppy ears,

I'd surely purr
and **hum.**

A **hatch** that's full
of water and **hay,**

Would **cheerfully**
fill my tum.

If I could be a pet,
I'd be a BOX TURTLE.

My shell would be
an olive green,
shiny hard circle.

I'd wade in
shallow water.

And dine on
leafy greens.

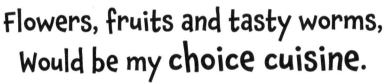

Flowers, fruits and tasty worms,
Would be my choice cuisine.

If I could be a **pet**,
I'd be a FLUFFY PUPPY.

I'd **chew** and **tug** my braided toy,
And nap beside our **guppy**.

I'd "sit" and "roll" for belly rubs.

And **dance** on paws for treats.

Woofing "HELLO" and "HOW ARE YOU?"

To **puppies** on my street.

If I could be a pet,
I'd be a GOLDEN HAMSTER.

Playing hide and seek each day,
I'd be the family prankster.

I'd **climb** the rails
inside my **house.**

And run **fast**
around my **wheel.**

Rolling in my hamster ball,
Would surely make me **squeal!**

If I could be a pet,
I'd be a PERSIAN KITTEN.

My cute and playful kisses,
Could make a house mouse smitten.

I'd **prance** around so **gracefully**
and chase my **jingly** toys.

Hiding, climbing,
taking naps,

Are things that I'd **enjoy**.

But as I sit and wonder
Of how **different** I could be,
I quickly come to realize
That it's special to be ME!

With **hands** to clap,

a **mouth** to smile,

a pair of **eyes** to see.

All placed differently
But oh so **PERFECTLY**,
Making ME, uniquely ME.

So today I will **appreciate**
Pets on land and sea.

I'll care for **pets** the best I can,
And keep on being **ME!**

What Readers are Saying

My Kids Love It!
Such a cute idea for a book. My kids are always running around pretending to be different animals. They loved this! We read it and talked about what it would be like to be each pet. Very cute story. Would recommend to all my mom friends!!

-Heather S.

My son wants to be a turtle!
This book is a fantastic short read for my preschool age son and I to enjoy. When I asked him what pet he would like to be for one day, he replied with "A turtle! Because I love to swim!" We like to learn the fun facts and traits of pets in an age appropriate context. Buy this book for the curious pet loving children in your life!

-Amazon Customer

Thoughtfully written children's book!
I absolutely love the message and story telling of "If I Could ... Be A Pet!". It is creative, the illustrations are engaging and the rhyming makes it a fun read for all ages. A great gift for all the little ones in your life!

-Maggie S.

What pet would you be?
LOVE LOVE LOVE!!! A cute story about a sweet little boy dreaming of what it would be like to be a pet. Although being a pet is special in many ways, the boy realizes he is just as special being himself. This book is brilliant on many levels. The illustrations are absolutely stunning and the clever rhyming makes this a fantastic, catchy read. Highly recommend!

-Bakon Brands

About the Author

Shona Darin is the author and owner of Library on Linwood; a Michigan children's book imprint. Shona's writing journey was fueled by her son's love of literature at a young age. During her time at home raising her sons, she found that her creative outlet was writing short children's stories. This hobby soon snowballed into a passion project which she is thrilled to share with the world.

To support Shona's journey or to buy her book directly, please follow @libraryonlinwood on Instagram and Facebook or visit www.libraryonlinwood.com.

About the Illustator

Anne Zimanski is a freelance illustrator, with a passion for all things creative! She has illustrated dozens of children's books and works in a wide range of digital and traditional art styles. Anne resides in Northern Michigan with her husband and daughter, and when not working she loves to travel and explore new places.

To see more of Anne's illustration work, please follow @az.illustration on instagram, or visit www.annezimanski.com.